GOOD NIGHT, GORILLA

Peggy Rathmann

EGMONT

Good night, Gorilla.

GORILLA

ZOO
JOE

Good night, Elephant.

Good night, Lion.

Good night, Hyena.
Good night, Giraffe.

Good night, Armadillo.

ZOO

Good night, dear.

Good night.
Good night.
Good night.

Good night.

Good night.

Good night.

Good night.

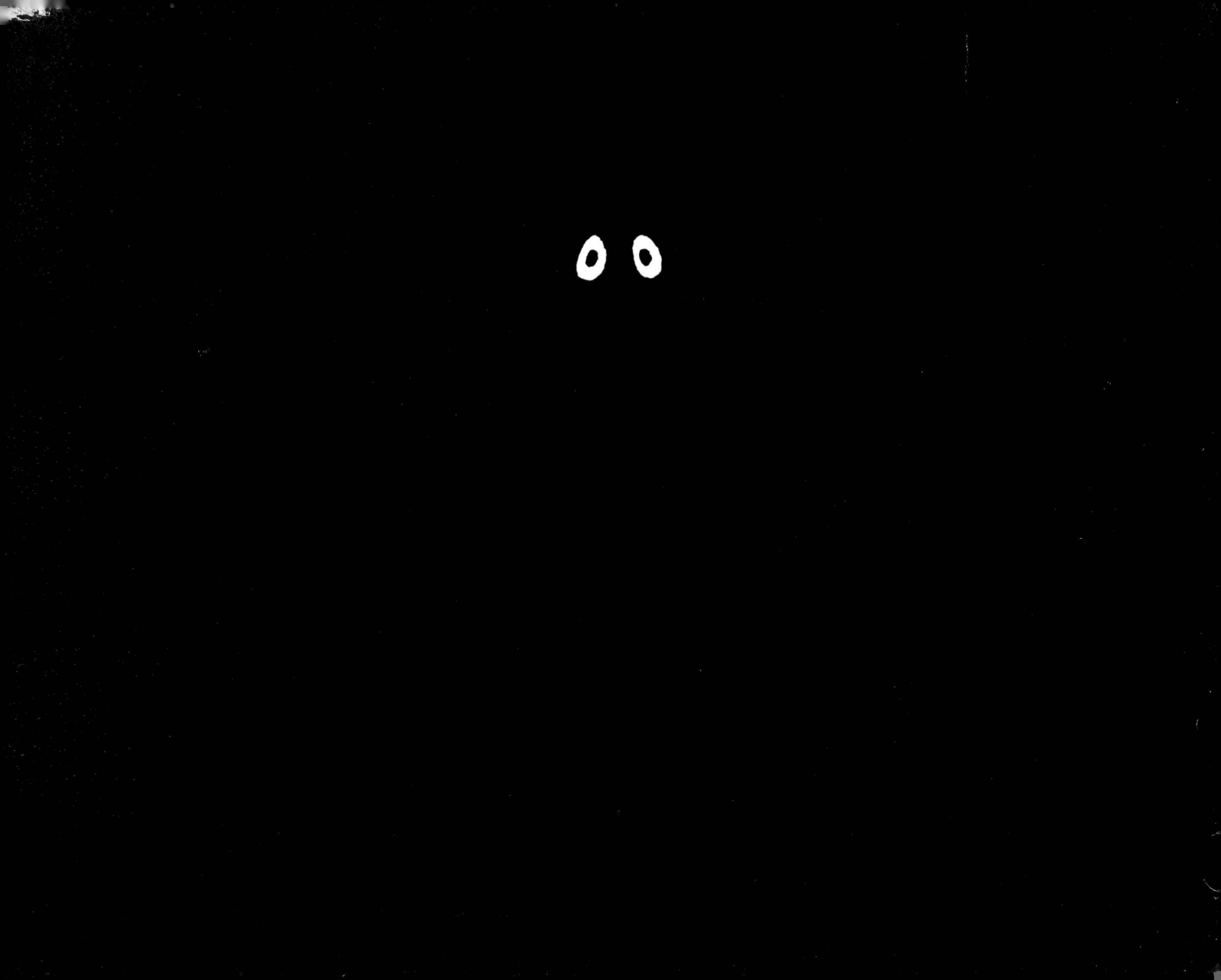

ZOOKEEPER

ZOO

ZOOKEEPER

Good night, zoo.

Good night, dear.
Good night.